JOHNY IS BIRD BOY

Written by FARAH AMBRIN

Illustrated by Dennis Davide

To order additional copies of this book, contact:
Xlibris
0800-056-3182
www.xlibrispublishing.co.uk
Orders@ Xlibrispublishing.co.uk

ISBN: Softcover   978-1-9845-9328-3
         EBook   978-1-9845-9327-6

Print information available on the last page

Rev. date: 15/01/2020

THE MIRACLE OF SAVING A LIFE

Story 1

Johny was always bored. You see he had **no brothers** to play with. That's the reason why or so Johny thought, "there is **nothing to do in the house**".

"I'm booorrred!" he moaned with a fake coughing sort of crying sound, wriggling and jiggling his joints and stamping of his feet.

"ok so why don't you go and **clean** your room then?" his mother suggested.

She thought that was a good way to distract him from his boredom and give him something to do.

"I want to go out somewhere!" he pulled at his mom's dress. "you can go and **play in the garden** or you can play with the **vacuum cleaner!** which one do you choose?" said his mother.

she did that sometimes turn the vacuum on and give it to Johny who didn't realize that he was cleaning as he pushed it around.

OOOOOooo! He said as he pushed it around. "Move out of the way everybody the eating monster is coming!" The vacuum cleaner sucked up everything in its path.

Johny's mom thought it was clever.

"There is nothing to do in the garden" he moaned. "get me a brother to play with! It's not fair! My friend Michael has four brothers! why did you get me three sister's and no brothers!". He wailed.

Johny's sisters chirped from the sitting room where they were brushing their dolls hair and setting up pretty little furniture in a beautiful pink dolls house.

"because she liked girls moore so she brought three of them, and she didn't like boys that much so she only brought one". "muuum!" wailed Johny. "did you hear that!"

"Rosie! That's not true, you don't get to choose whether you have a boy baby or a girl baby, you just have to take what you are given" tried to explain their mother. Johny imagined taking a shopping trolley around a supermarket and there were rows of smiling baby boys sitting on shelves holding their arms out asking to be picked. It couldn't have been difficult choosing more baby boys, he thought.

"Take me!" he pleaded "please! I will choose for you. I will say three more baby boys please!". Johny tugged on his mother's skirt as she held her head in her hands.

Realizing his mother was not going to listen to him.

He picked up his football and went to the garden. Moaning as he went "who do I kick this ball to! Tell me! I need someone to kick it back to meee! aaarraah!"

Unfortunately, Johny's two older sisters Rosie and Jerry were very girly. They liked sparkly things and dolls with long hair and pretty dresses. They loved to dress up playing with make-up and jewellery and could happily comb and braid their dolls hair for hours.

Johny's mother had told him she was going to get him a brother but had come back with his littlest sister Cat, who was younger than him. That's when Johny really did believe that she did like girls more than boys. How can you go to get a boy baby and come back with a girl baby? That's what he wanted to know.

His little sister Cat loved sucking dummies and collecting them too. They were coming out of everywhere. His mother was in despair. Johny was happy though because they kept her quiet.

Johny had liked all those things too until he had learned that he was a boy and boys were supposed to play with cars and football's and love getting mucky. With two older sisters he was born with pink all around him. As for sucking dummies he had done that too, until his mother had sat with him at the table with a pair of scissors and cut the rubber that you suck off them! and when he had wailed, she had handed him all the hard-plastic backs. His mother, thought Johny needed to do that again to his little sister Cat who looked like a cat too crawling around the house.

Outside he gave the ball an **enormous kick**. Sending it flying up in the air and landing into the tree at the back of the garden. The ball rustled through the leaves and branches and slowly a **baby bird** started to fall out, Johny ran under the tree catching it just before it hit the floor.

Wow, he thought. **A baby bird!** Unbeknown to him the bird's mother had not returned to the nest. The poor thing had been caught under a car and been run over and in a flurry of feathers it was gone. The baby bird in the nest was very hungry and had not been fed and if it had not been for Johny it would not have even been discovered at all and surely it would have died of starvation.

Johny sensed the bird was hungry as it chirped weakly to him. He settled the baby bird in a cardboard box with lots of straw. Then he dug around looking for little **worms and insects.** Feeding and playing with the bird kept him very busy and out of his mother's way who dared not ask what was keeping him quiet.

He kept the baby bird a secret from his sisters. It was his and they were not going to be allowed to see it or play with it. Certainly not if he couldn't play with their dolls because he was a boy! **"boys don't play with dolls; boys play with cars"** they chorused together. Johny had been annoyed at his mother "why didn't you tell me I was a boy!" The boys had laughed at him when he had started nursery. "Boys don't play with dolls they play with cars!" they too had said. So, he had come home and thrown his beloved dolls across the room. He knew he was a boy now! And he wanted to be a proper boy. Not one that played with girl's toys but one that played with boy's toys. "oh dear" sighed his mom, he had admired the dolls from the moment he saw them.

Johny kept an eye out for the mommy bird to return and seeing when she didn't come, he sneaked the baby bird into his room for **warmth and safety.**

Keeping the baby bird silent was difficult and he was worried his secret will be discovered. He had to make sure his mom did not come in his bedroom. So, he went about cleaning it, like she had asked him to. He proudly called his mom to see what a good job he had done and told her "no one must enter my room in case they mess it up, not even when I go to school". "don't even open the door in case germs fly in" he told his mother. Who was very puzzled? this was not her Johny. Had his boredom caused him to clean up? She certainly was not complaining if some good had come out of it and he had been so quiet for once. She was over the moon; she was so happy she thought she could hear birds tweeting when really it was the baby bird in Johny's room. Finally, Johny had found a passion. Cleaning. Who would have thought of it!

Johny couldn't wait to get home from school so instead of holding his mum's hand and walking sensibly he ran ahead leaving her rushing to keep up with him, he had to feed his baby. It was not long before the baby bird had grown strong and Johny trained it to fly by giving it little goals. Like flying from the wardrobe onto the bed and then flying from the bed onto the floor and then back up again. Flying upwards was always more difficult for the baby bird then flying downwards and sometimes Johny would end up giving it a helping hand to fly to the top. He would sneak it into the bathroom and let it bath in the sink, treating the slow running tap like a mini shower and then he would carry it back to his bedroom wrapped in a fluffy yellow towel. The little yellow chick changed colour and grew into a little blue bird. It started to flap its wings and jump and fly around his room. Johny was like a proud mother. As the bird flew a dance around him his eyes welled up with tears, it was time to open the window and let it fly away. To leave the nest of Johny's bedroom and create a natural life for itself.

It was exactly at this moment a miracle took place. Johny had performed an act of great kindness. He had saved a life! however small it was and surely every act of kindness deserved to be rewarded. So, as the bird kissed him on the nose his feet lifted off the floor and he started to fly with the bird in his bedroom. Amazed and delighted he opened the window and they both flew out together. Up and around and over the house's, they somersaulted and rolled in the air. With the beak facing up they fly high and then they faced the beak down and spread their wing's and sailed down through the sky. Johny laughed, oh what fun! and then they joined an arrow of dancing birds and Johny took the lead. Until he got tired and then dropped to the back of the flock. Gently he dropped behind, back and back.

He lifted a hand to say **goodbye** as the little bird looked back, and it was there. He left the bird with them, where it belonged. Back he flew, people who looked up to the sky said **is it a bird? Is it a plane?**

Johny flew back inside through his bedroom window. Had it all been a dream? He tried again and he could still fly! Now what Johny needed was a costume and he had a perfect idea. He didn't need dolls or even brothers anymore. He was going to make a costume, **complete with a sack of droppings!**

BIRDBOY IS BORN

Story 2

Johny has discovered a new game. Flying down the stairs and then flying back up the stairs and as he was about to fly back down the stairs, he heard his sister's footsteps approaching and quickly he landed himself on his feet and cheerfully he walked down the stairs whistling to himself proudly with his chin up in the air. Rosie thought his smile looked smug, the same as when he had sneaked into her bedroom and eaten her birthday chocolates. He was definitely up to something she thought giving him a curious look as she walked past.

She definitely didn't fall for the cleaning story, that definitely was not like Johny. Mom had told them all not to open Johny's bedroom door because he was worried the germs would fly in. When Johny was downstairs, she sneaked into his bedroom. She quickly shuffled through his things but she didn't find anything other than the empty cardboard box with some straw in it and a single yellow feather floated out of it. Disappointed she left his room.

Downstairs Johny didn't annoy his mother anymore, he didn't moan that he was bored. He said he wanted to play by himself. In fact, now his mother thought he had taken to arts and crafts because he was looking for fabric's and scissors and asked if there was any glue and he was carrying feathers! Johny had taken the feather boa's off the old Easter bonnets! What a funny child thought his mother laughing to herself.

Then at dinner Johny asked if he could have more peas, His father gasped in shock and nearly choked on his food. Coughing he asked Johny to repeat what he had said. After he had finished them, he asked for more. His mother got up to check if Johny had a temperature, this was a new Johny, now he liked peas! After dinner she checked under the table to see if he had thrown them there as that's what he used to do, he always had to be told to finish his greens. But no there was not a single pea on the floor. His mother was pleased.

At bedtime Johny asked to go to bed early he said he was very tired. Kissing his parent's goodnight and even his sisters he went to his bedroom.

Once there he set about cutting and gluing until he had created a lovely **bird costume!** sticking the yellow feathers all over it and then **tah dah!** he pulled out the hidden peas. He had carefully hidden them away in a plastic bag and he mushed them up and mixed them up with water and created a little pouch in the costume and poured it in. Delighted with himself, he had created a perfect costume with a **bird droppings launcher!** He couldn't wait.

Tomorrow he was going to try it out.

Johny woke up early and he put the costume on. Flying out of the window he flew over the houses and gardens. He launched an attack of bird droppings on his next-door neighbour Margorie who was putting the washing out on the line, "oh! Oh!" she squealed. "a giant bird! Malcolm! Malcolm! Come quickly!" she called to her husband. Johny laughed, she always kept the balls that went over the fence. Then he launched the droppings at the early morning dog walkers as he flew over them. He laughed mischievously as he saw them hopping. Being naughty was so much fun.

He quickly flew back home before his mother would come in his room to wake him. He was looking forward to going to school today.

At playtime Johny flew above the playground the children looked up in aww "it's a boy! It's a boy!" they shouted, **"its Birdboy!"** He couldn't help but launch an attack of bird droppings on the school head master Mr.O'hair who was doing playground supervision. Landing droppings on his bald head! the naughty school children secretly called him Mr No'hair! he ran towards the school building for shelter, bird droppings ran down his glasses and a button popped on his shirt. **The children laughed.** Everyone knew whenever there was any danger Mr O'hair was always the first to run away from it. When Johny flew over the school bully's, he launched droppings at them. The kids cheered and laughed.

Birdboy set off a new craze. Theme parks were created with Birdboy themed rides and the toy shops were bustling. All the boys wanted the costume. Boys ran around wearing bird beak face masks and bird claw slippers and were shooting with plastic hand held dropping launchers. Boys and girls were wearing Birdboy wings and carrying Birdboy figures with flapping wings and parents were bringing home Birdcage palace dolls houses just for boys! and Johny's house was full of them. Now it was his sisters who kept playing with boy's toys.

The school held a non-uniform day and all the boys came dressed as Birdboy. Johny went to school dressed in his actual costume and no one knew that he was the real **Birdboy**. As all the other Birdboy's ran around the playground it was just him who was flying above, launching droppings as he flew and just to show his mischievous side, he couldn't help but land one again on the fat principles bald head. "haha" he laughed. "you won't guess which bird did it this time!" with dropping launchers going off everywhere the playground was getting a bit mucky and as the principle ran, he slipped and just barely regained his balance to save his fall.

At home Johny was no longer bored he had his toys and he allowed his sisters to play with them.

THE NAUGHTY BIRD

Story 3

Johny flew above shooting his bird dropping launcher randomly. Targeting the droppings at car windscreens and laughing as the car washers came on and swished the windows clean again. Spreading his wings wide he **swooshed** and glided through the air.

Johny has become famous and has now earned himself the name of naughty bird. In fact, news had got to the queen about this naughty bird and So she was soon going to summon for the bird to be caught and brought to her. Giant nets were being prepared to catch the naughty bird and a giant bird cage had been prepared. There were newspaper headlines saying has **Birdboy gotten too big for his cage?** So, as Johny went about his mischief for the time being he had no idea. At the moment when kids see him flying, they wait in excitement for something naughty to happen.

He quietly fly's over a lady wearing an apron and gently lifts the wig she is wearing and fly's off leaving her covering her bald head with the mop she was carrying. The kids laugh, then Johny fly's off to find more mischief.

He lands in a garden with a bird feeding table and perches his feet on it making the stand snap and break and bird seeds scatter out of it as it falls. The naughty bird is far heavier than an actual bird. He fly's away leaving the man in the garden waving his arms angrily at him.

Johny was having so much fun being a nuisance that he didn't realize what time it was, his mum at home had tea ready on the table and was looking for him shouting "Johny! Where are you" she had looked everywhere couldn't find him, luckily he landed home just in time for her to look outside "oh there you are she said as he peered from around the corner of the shed. "come here look at your hair how messy it is" she gently patted it on his head as he came to her. "I love you mom" he said to her sweetly. His mum hugged him lovingly. "I love you to" and he smiled mischievously while his mom could not see his face.

On the table his mom had a large bowl of peas for him, "mmmm" he said "and I love peas too".

Printed in the United States
By Bookmasters